STRONG AS A BEAR

for
Helene

enchantedlionbooks.com

First American edition published in 2016 by Enchanted Lion Books,
351 Van Brunt Street, Brooklyn, NY 11231
Adapted from the German by Claudia Bedrick
Copyright © 2016 by Enchanted Lion for the English-language text
Layout of US Edition: Marc Drumwright, Sarah Klinger
Originally published in Germany in 2013 as *Stark Wie Ein Bär*
Copyright © 2013 for text and illustrations by Aladin-Verlag, GmbH
A CIP record is on file with the Library of Congress
ISBN 978-1-59270-198-8
Printed in China by RR Donnelley Asia Printing Solutions Ltd.
10 9 8 7 6 5 4 3 2 1

KATRIN STANGL

STRONG
AS A
BEAR

ENCHANTED LION BOOKS

NEW YORK

FREE AS A BIRD

QUICK AS A HARE

LOUD AS A ROOSTER

MISCHIEVOUS AS A MONKEY

QUIET AS A MOUSE

SHY AS A DEER

BIG AS AN ELEPHANT

HUNGRY AS A WOLF

SLOW AS A SNAIL

RED AS A LOBSTER

ANGRY AS A BULL

BRAVE AS A LION

SLOPPY AS A PIG

SILENT AS A FISH

WILD AS A TIGER

CLEVER AS A FOX

ELEGANT AS A SWAN

SELFISH AS A MAGPIE

THIRSTY AS A CAMEL

BUSY AS A BEE

CURIOUS AS A CAT

STRONG AS A BEAR

PROUD AS A PEACOCK

STUBBORN AS A MULE

CHATTY AS A COCKATOO

PILLOWY AS A POODLE